Penny-Farthing Productions Presents

AUDREY'S MAGIC NINE

Created by
Courtney Huddleston

Written by
Michelle Wright

Art by
Courtney Huddleston
&
Francesco Gerbino

Colors by
Tracy Bailey

Letters by
André McBride

Chapter One

Approval

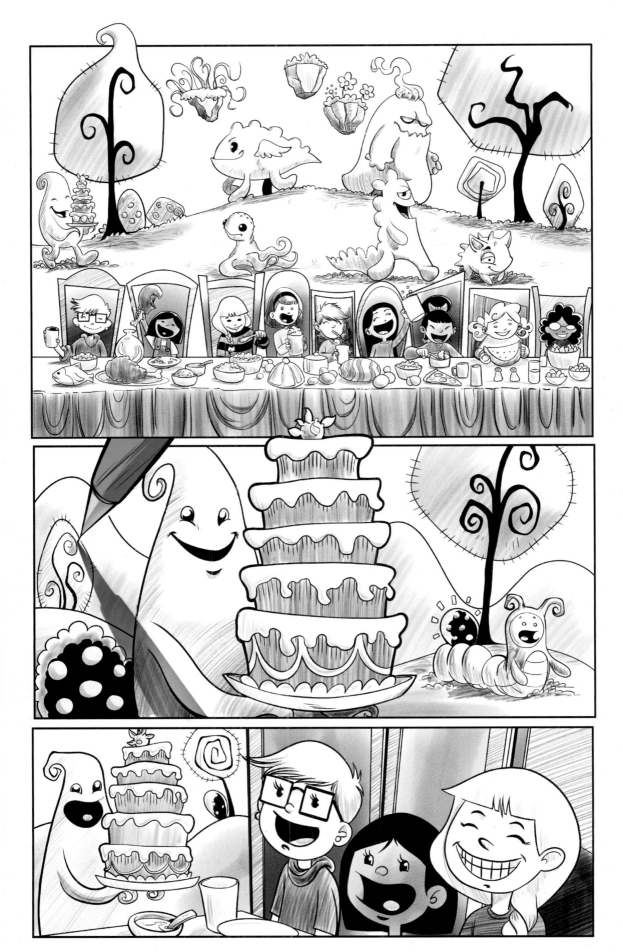

MERCER FAMILY FOSTER HOME.

HURRY! THEY'LL BE BACK SOON.

I AM HURRYING.

WHAT HAPPENS WHEN THEY DO GET HERE?

THEY'RE GONNA NOTICE THAT THE FOOD IS GONE.

WELL, WE'LL DEAL WITH THE SITUATION WHEN THE TIME COMES.

YOU'RE HUNGRY NOW, AREN'T YOU?

GOT IT!

CHINK

THEY'LL PUT US IN *THE CLOSET.*

THE LAST TIME I WAS IN THE CLOSET, I—

IF ANYONE GOES IN THE CLOSET, IT'LL BE ME.

BUT, YOU KNOW HOW *THEY* ARE.

AUDREY.

DON'T LOSE OUT.

I KNOW HOW THEY ARE, BUT THEY CAN'T GET AWAY WITH BARELY FEEDING US.

BUT THEY HAVE GOTTEN AWAY WITH IT. WE'RE JUST FOSTER KIDS...JUST GOVERNMENT CHECKS TO THEM.

WELL, THINGS ARE GOING TO CHANGE.

CRASH!

HEY!

SSSSHINK

GASP

WELL, HELLO!

OHHHH, I LOVE WHAT YOU'VE DRAWN!

I USED TO BE AN ARTIST, TOO. MAY I SEE YOUR BOOK?

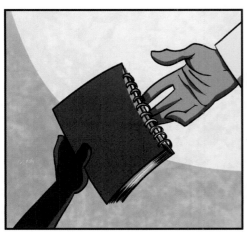

SO, THE REFRIGERATOR WAS LOCKED.

HEY, JOE?

YEAH?

RUN AROUND THE CORNER. GET ANOTHER NOTE BOOK *JUST LIKE THIS.*

I NEED TO KEEP THIS BOOK FOR NOW, BUT I'M GOING TO GET YOU ANOTHER ONE.

WHAT D'YA SAY WE BLOW THIS POPSICLE STAND?

THIS IS AUTUMN DESTINY, REPORTING LIVE FROM THE 600TH BLOCK OF MORIARTY AVENUE...

...WHERE SHOCKING LIVING CONDITIONS WERE DISCOVERED...

...AT WHAT SOME ARE DUBBING "THE LITTLE HOUSE OF FOSTER HOME HORRORS."

LIVE

FOSTER HOME HORROR

HINKLE HOME.

I AM BEING TOLD THAT OFFICERS ARE BRINGING OUT THE LAST OF THE CHILDREN.

THERE WERE SEVERAL YOUNG GIRLS IN THE MERCER FOSTERS HOME, RANGING IN AGES 5 TO 16...

...AND ALLEGEDLY SUBJECTED TO SUCH PUNISHMENTS AS HOURS SPENT IN A SMALL, LOCKED CLOSET.

...THIS IS TERRIBLE!

OH MY GOSH...

LADIES, ARE YOU SEEING THIS?

THESE PEOPLE WERE LOCKING CHILDREN... CHILDREN...IN A CLOSET... FOR HOURS!

WHOA!

12

SNICKER

YES, TABITHA, THAT IS CERTAINLY...

...<AHEM>... DISTURBING.

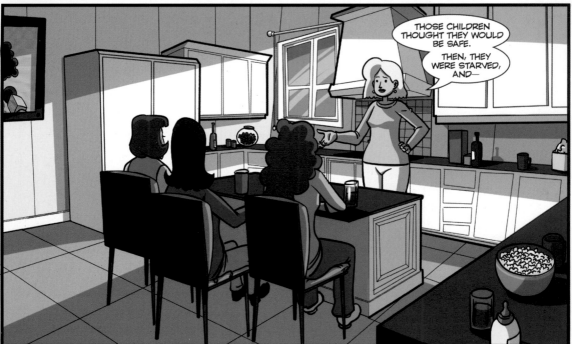

THOSE CHILDREN THOUGHT THEY WOULD BE SAFE.

THEN, THEY WERE STARVED, AND—

OH, I FEEL ANOTHER ONE OF TABITHA'S SPECIAL CAUSES COMING ON.

AWWW... THAT'S SO SWEET.

SHE CERTAINLY LIKES TO EAT SWEETS.

NEVER MIND.

IT'S NOT THAT BIG OF A DEAL.

SO...SHOPPING... YEAH!!

NOW, WAIT A MINUTE.

I THINK YOU MIGHT BE ONTO SOMETHING.

REALLY?

OF COURSE. WE ALL KNOW YOU CAN'T HAVE CHILDREN.

SOOO...TAB—

HEY, MAY I CALL YOU TABBY? I HAD A DOG NAMED "TABBY" WHEN I WAS A KID. "TABITHA" IS JUST SUCH A MOUTH FULL.

SURE.

ANYWAY, CONSIDERING YOUR SITUATION AND ALL...

...AND YOUR...OH, I DON'T KNOW WHAT YOU WOULD CALL IT...YOUR HOBBY...FOR HELPING PEOPLE...

...YOU SHOULD ADOPT ONE OF THOSE KIDS.

15

DO YOU THINK JONATHAN WOULD GO FOR IT?

JONATHAN HINKLE.

DINKLE, HOW DO YOU MESS UP GRILLING *BURGERS*?

...IT'S HINKLE...

LOSER MOVE MAN!

YEAH. HE'LL GO FOR IT.

OH, OF COURSE. WE--

MR. AND MRS. HINKLE...?

...WHAT DO YOU SEE?

DO YOU SEE HAPPY CHILDREN?

NO.

NOW YOU SEE SOMETHING DIFFERENT.

YOU SEE A CHILD WHO HAS NOT LET THIS SYSTEM BEAT HER.

I HAVE HAD HIGH HOPES FOR THIS CHILD.

NONE OF WHICH HAVE COME TO PASS.

THIS *MUST* WORK OUT FOR *AUDREY.*

DO YOU UNDERSTAND?

YES.

WE UNDERSTAND. WE ARE GOING TO GIVE AUDREY OPPORTUNITIES THAT WE DIDN'T HAVE IN THIS WORLD.

YES, WE WANT HER TO HAVE CHANCES TO SHINE.

AUDREY *ALREADY* SHINES.

ALL RIGHT...

...WE WILL SEE YOU TOMORROW.

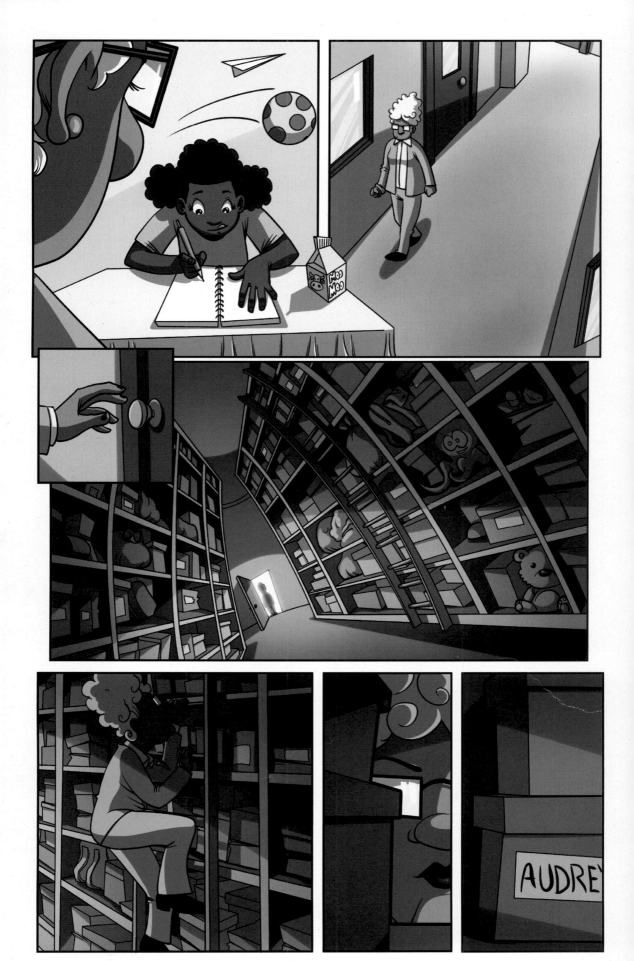

NO, MY DEAR, YOU AREN'T IN TROUBLE.

I HAVE SOME GOOD NEWS FOR YOU.

YOU'VE BEEN ADOPTED.

NOW, DON'T LOOK AT ME THAT WAY.

I REALLY THINK THIS IS THE RIGHT PLACE FOR YOU.

THIS IS A REAL HOME...

...A FOREVER HOME.

YOU WERE ALWAYS ONE OF MY FAVORITES.

NO MATTER WHAT THIS PLACE THREW AT YOU, YOU NEVER BACKED DOWN. I WANT YOU TO STAY THAT WAY.

LOOK WHAT I FOUND. HE WAS MIXED IN WITH ALL YOUR NOTE BOOKS.

OF COURSE, I'VE KEPT ALL YOUR NOTE BOOKS. HOW COULD I NOT KEEP SUCH ITEMS OF BEAUTY?

GOOD LUCK, AUDREY.

Chapter Two
The Sound And The Fuzzy

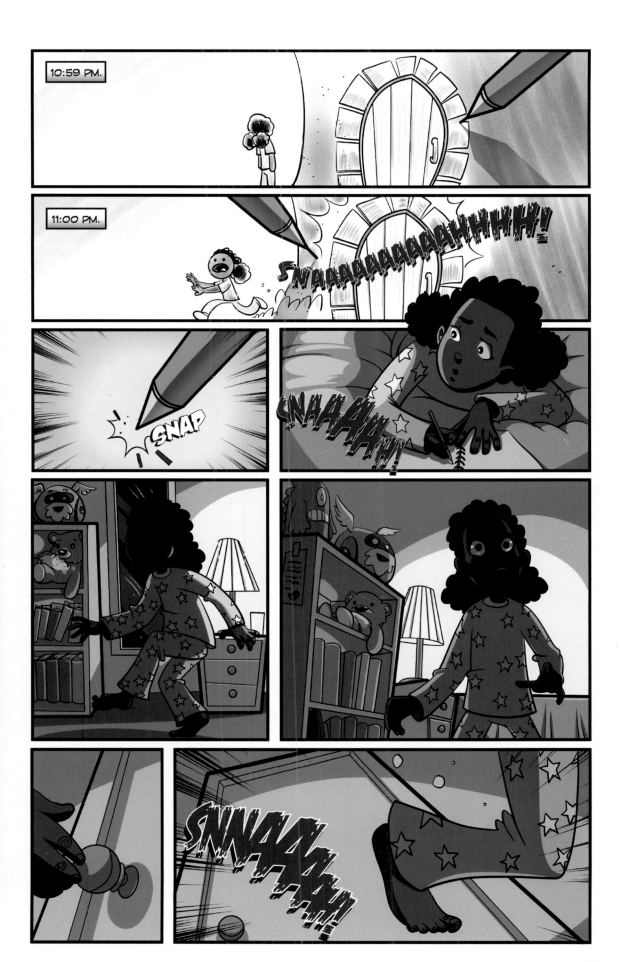

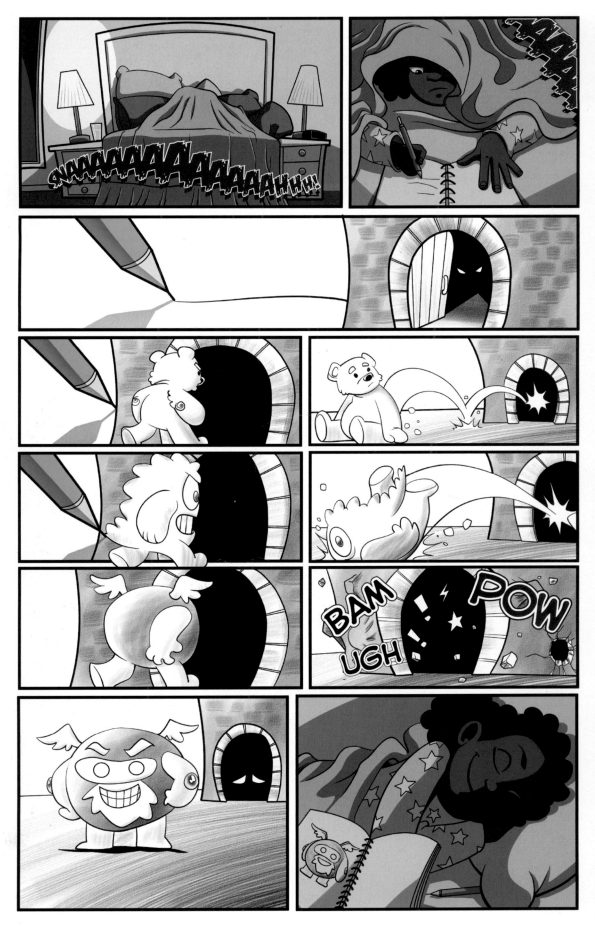

AUDREY...

...TIME TO—

AUDREY! ARE YOU OK?

OH, AUDREY....

DID YOU GET SCARED?

WHEN I WAS A LITTLE GIRL, I USED TO THINK THAT A RABID PIXIE LIVED UNDER MY BED--

BUT THAT'S NEITHER HERE NOR THERE.

ARE YOU READY TO START YOUR *EXCELLENT* LIFE?

FIRST THING, COACH BARRET HAS AGREED TO MEET YOU AT 7:30 BEFORE SCHOOL SO YOU CAN GET CAUGHT UP WITH THE SOCCER TEAM. YOU NEED TO WORK ON PASSING.

NEXT, SINCE YOU TESTED SO WELL AT YOUR LAST SCHOOL, YOU ARE GOING TO BE IN THE ACCELERATED PROGRAM HERE. JONATHAN AND I ARE ACTUALLY HOPING YOU WILL BE ABLE TO SKIP A GRADE.

ALSO, I WAS THINKING YOU'VE BEEN CALLING ME MRS. HINKLE AND IF YOU'RE COMFORTABLE WITH IT, YOU CAN CALL ME TABITHA...

OR...MOM?

FIFTEEN MINUTES LATER.

I THINK I'LL JUST CALL YOU TABITHA FOR NOW, IF THAT'S OK.

SURE, THAT WORKS!

NEXT, YOU HAVE BALLET RIGHT AFTER SCHOOL. YOU WILL HAVE BALLET EVERY DAY TO BUILD UP TO DANCING *EN POINTE* FOR ALL THOSE MAIN ROLES IN RECITALS.

THEN, YOU WILL HAVE PIANO LESSONS WITH MR. STANFLIE. I HEAR HE IS THE BEST—AN ACTUAL CONCERT PIANIST.

NOW, THAT IS *ONLY* MONDAY.

ON TUESDAY, MEET WITH COACH BARRET, SCHOOL, BALLET, AND THEN...SHOULD WE LET HER GUESS, JONATHAN?

STARTS WITH A "V".

A BOW, STRINGS...A SOUND SO BEAUTIFUL IT MAKES GROWN MEN WEEP... WELL THIS GROWN MAN AT LEAST.

JONATHAN...DON'T LET ANYONE HEAR YOU SAY THAT—ESPECIALLY NOT THE KEENANS!

WELL, OF COURSE NOT.

CAN YOU GUESS, AUDREY?

UHHHHHHH....

IT'S A *VIOLIN*, SILLY.

I WOULD'VE DONE ANYTHING TO BE ABLE TO PLAY THE VIOLIN!

ON WEDNESDAY...

...YOU ALREADY KNOW THE FIRST PART...SOCCER, SCHOOL, BALLET...

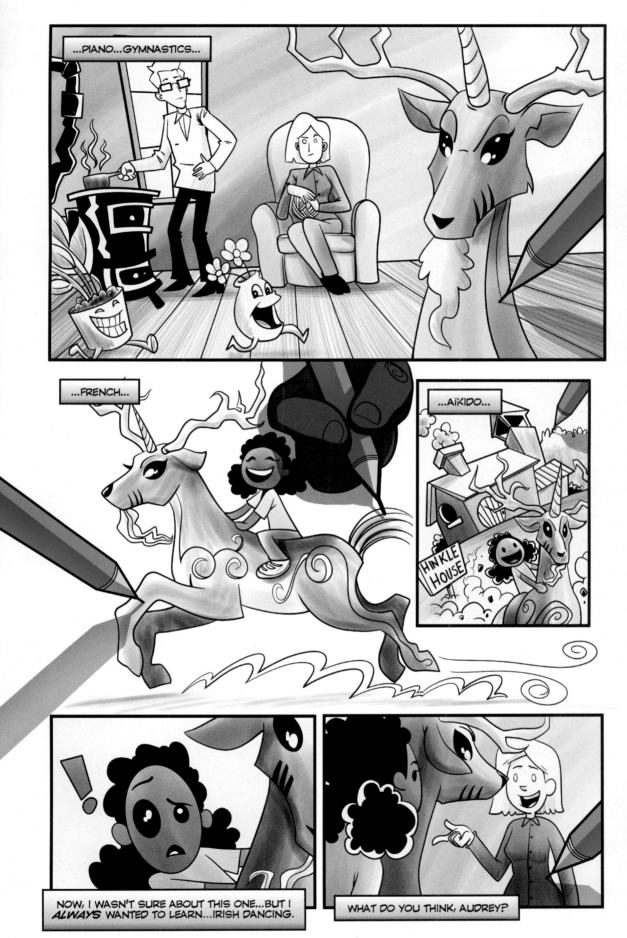

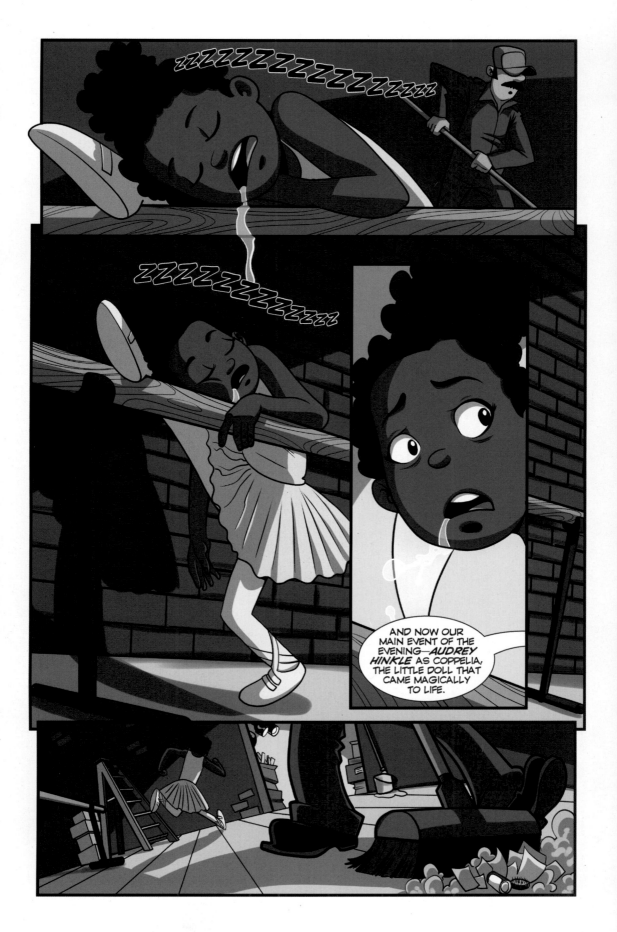

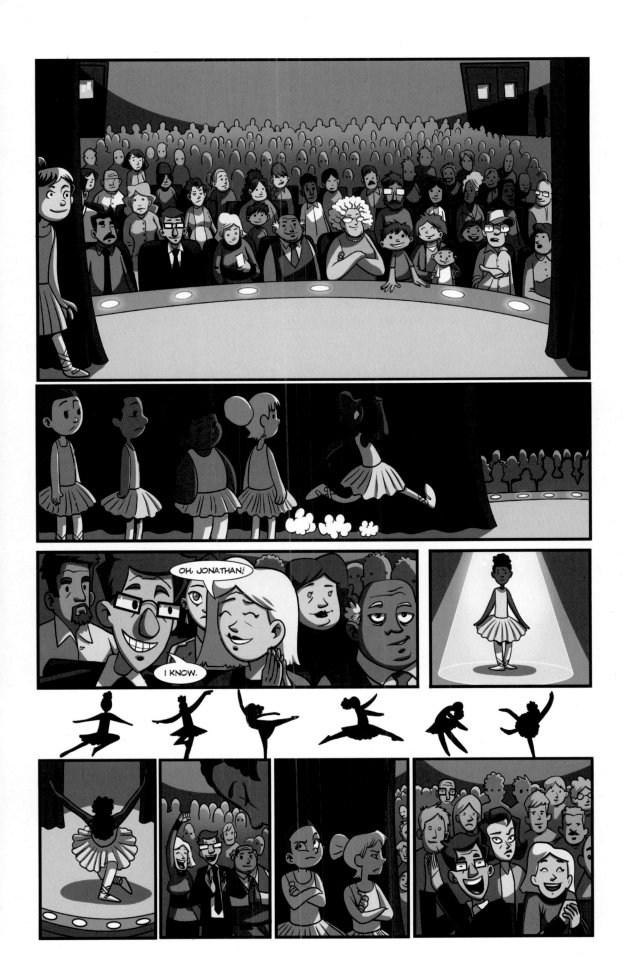

WE ARE *IN.*

AND THAT CONCLUDES TONIGHT'S PROGRAM. PLEASE JOIN US FOR WINE AND HORS D'OEUVRES TO CELEBRATE THESE LOVELY YOUNG LADIES IN THE GREEN ROOM.

SO, WHAT DID YOU THINK?

PRETTY AMAZING, HUH?

WELL...

...I MEAN...

IT WAS ACTUALLY *VERY* GOOD. BUT THEY CAN'T KNOW THAT.

...IT WAS CERTAINLY....

...INTERESTING. YES, THAT'S IT: INTERESTING.

YOU KNOW, JUST HAVE HER KEEP PRACTICING FIVE DAYS A WEEK—MAYBE SATURDAYS TOO FOR THE NEXT, SAY FOUR, MAYBE FIVE YEARS...AND THEN...WE'LL SEE.

BEAUTIFUL.

MARVELOUS.

WAS I OK?

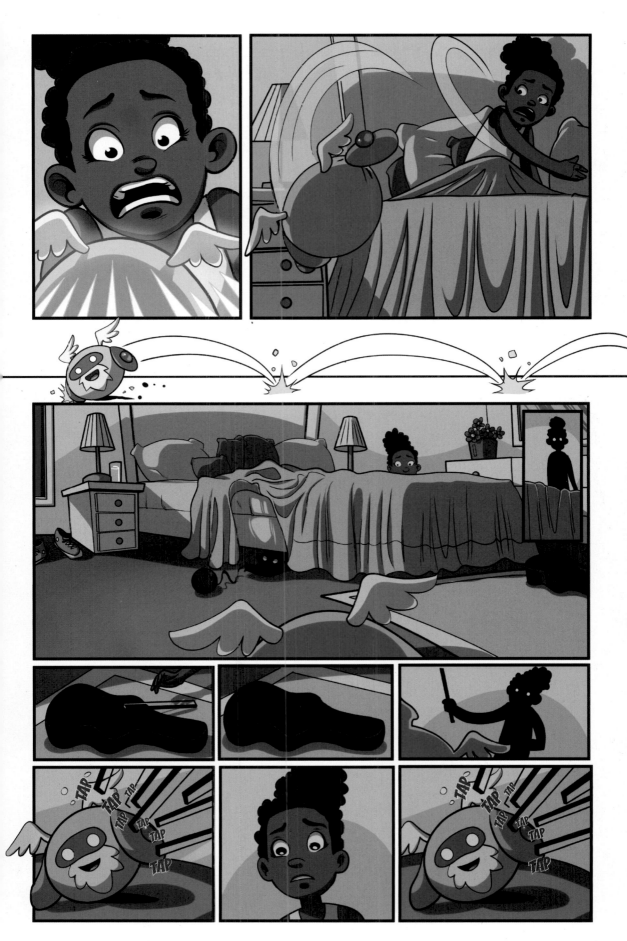

IT COULD BE WORSE.

YOU COULD HAVE A HAND UP YOUR— SNAAAAAAA

WHAT THE FERGUS WAS THAT?

IT SHAKES THE VERY GROUND.

HOW ARE YOU ABLE TO SPEAK?

LET'S GRAB SOME COVER, AND WE'LL TALK.

I KNOW WHERE WE WILL BEGIN...WITH A STORY OF...

BATTLE!

YOU KNOW, THERE WAS A TIME, WHEN I WOULDN'T TOLERATE A NOISE LIKE THAT—MOST LIKELY MADE BY SOME DAFT GUMPTY—JUST SPOILING FOR A FIGHT.

SMACK

ONE TIME, THIS MARSH DOBBER WENT OFF OF HIS HEAD SO LOUD THAT MY CLAN—THE MIGHTY ZEPHYRS—HEARD IT ALL THE WAY UP FEOGAN PEAK.

IT JUST WANTED TO ANNOY SOMEBODY.

AND HE DID!

I TOOK IT ALMOST AS FAR AS THE MARSHES.

ALMOST.

BLEET?

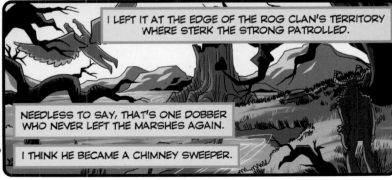

I LEFT IT AT THE EDGE OF THE ROG CLAN'S TERRITORY WHERE STERK THE STRONG PATROLLED.

NEEDLESS TO SAY, THAT'S ONE DOBBER WHO NEVER LEFT THE MARSHES AGAIN.

I THINK HE BECAME A CHIMNEY SWEEPER.

YOU SEE, VORGON, WAS RIPE WITH MAGICIANS, VERY POWERFUL ONES WHO WIELDED THEIR MAGIC WITH GREAT FORCE.

BUT THEY UNDERSTOOD THAT SUCH A PLACE AS OUR WORLD WITH ITS CLANS AND LANDMASSES AND—OH! THE MAGIC OF EVERYDAY PEOPLE—COULDN'T BE RULED FAIRLY BY THOSE WITH STRONGER ABILITIES.

PEOPLE HAD BEEN KILLED ACCIDENTALLY BY MAGICIANS, YOU SEE, AND THOSE WISE MAGES WOULD NOT SEEK POWER FOR THAT REASON.

INSTEAD, THEY PROPOSED THAT THE WORLD BE GOVERNED BY REPRESENTATIVES CHOSEN FROM THE NINE MAJOR CLANS AND OFFERED THEIR COUNSEL ONLY.

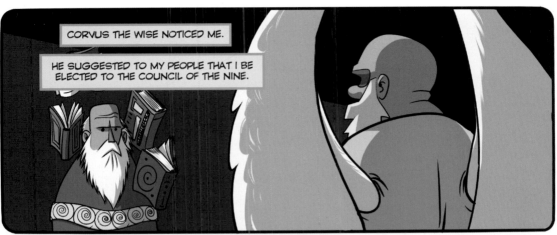

CORVUS THE WISE NOTICED ME.

HE SUGGESTED TO MY PEOPLE THAT I BE ELECTED TO THE COUNCIL OF THE NINE.

AND MY PEOPLE CHOSE ME UNANIMOUSLY.

THE COUNCIL WORKED WELL...UNTIL...

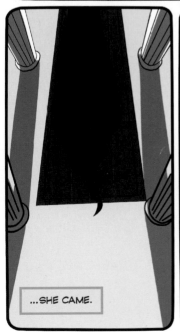

...SHE CAME.

SHE CAME OUT OF NOWHERE, RISING AMONG THE MAGICIANS. SHE GAINED A FOLLOWING DURING A TIME OF STRIFE. SHE SET THINGS RIGHT, THOUGH, SUPPORTED THE COUNCIL OF NINE AND THE MAGICIANS.

AND THEN SHE CROWNED HERSELF QUEEN, DISMANTLING EVERYTHING THAT HAD TAKEN CENTURIES TO BUILD.

SHE CHANGED VORGON.

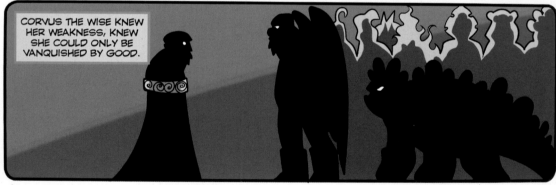

CORVUS THE WISE KNEW HER WEAKNESS, KNEW SHE COULD ONLY BE VANQUISHED BY GOOD.

BUT THOSE WERE STRANGE TIMES.

AND THEN A STRANGER THING HAPPENED.

SOMEHOW A PORTAL OPENED BETWEEN VORGON AND YOUR WORLD.

WE DID NOT KNOW IF THE EVIL QUEEN WAS TO BLAME, BUT...

...WE WERE PULLED THROUGH THAT DOORWAY, DESPITE ALL OF CORVUS THE WISE'S EFFORT.

WE COULD DO NOTHING.

AND I, ASA, MIGHTY ASA, STRETCHED MY STRONG WINGS AS FAR AS THEY COULD REACH.

BUT I WAS NOT AS STRONG AS I THOUGHT.

I WAS DAFT TO THINK MYSELF SO.

WHEN I WOKE UP. I WAS LIKE YOU SEE ME NOW.

A PUPPET.

A PUPPET ALONE IN AN ALIEN PLACE...

...UNABLE TO EVEN EXERT ANY WILL OF MY OWN.

BUT NOW...NOW...THAT YOU AND I HAVE FOUND ONE ANOTHER...WE CAN CHANGE THAT.

YOU AND I CAN FIND THE OTHERS, REBUILD THE COUNCIL.

WE CAN GO HOME AND DEFEAT THE QUEEN.

WHAT ARE YOU DOING, LASS?

Chapter Three

Lessons In Moxie

MEMBERS ONLY COUNTRY CLUB.

SUNSET.

RUSTLE RUSTLE
RUSTLE RUSTLE

DID WE LOSE THEM?

YES!

RISE AND SHINE!

WE HAVE TO FIND THE REST OF THE NINE!

FIVE MORE MINUTES, LASS.

6:31 AM.

NO SOCCER, BALLET, PIANO, VIOLIN, VOICE, SCHOOL, OR AIKIDO.

I AM FREE TO FIND YOUR MAGIC FRIENDS!

SO, WHAT DO YOU REMEMBER SEEING FIRST ON EARTH?

COUGH COUGH COUGH

HACK HACK HACK

MMMPPPPRRRHHH

SOMETHING... <COUGH> ...BIG AND RED.

I KNOW EXACTLY WHERE TO START.

THERE'S A BIG RED SLIDE AT THE MEMBERS ONLY COUNTRY CLUB. THERE'S A LOT OF SECURITY GUARDS, BUT TABITHA AND JONATHAN ARE MEMBERS SO WE SHOULD BE FINE.

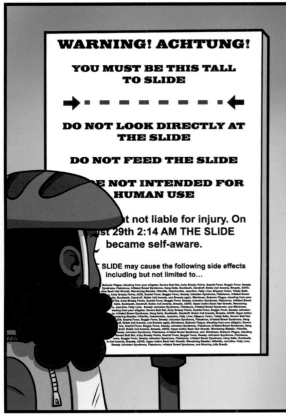

WARNING! ACHTUNG!

YOU MUST BE THIS TALL
TO SLIDE

➡ - ▪ - ▪ - ▪ - ▪ - ⬅

DO NOT LOOK DIRECTLY AT
THE SLIDE

DO NOT FEED THE SLIDE

E NOT INTENDED FOR
HUMAN USE

t not liable for injury. On
st 29th 2:14 AM THE SLIDE
became self-aware.

SLIDE may cause the following side effects
including but not limited to...

...BLINDNESS,
BUBONIC PLAGUE,
BLEEDING FROM
YOUR A—

WHOA!

MAY I BE
SPURNED BY ALL
THE CLANS OF VORGON
IF I SHOULD EVER SUFFER
SUCH A WOUND AS
THAT!

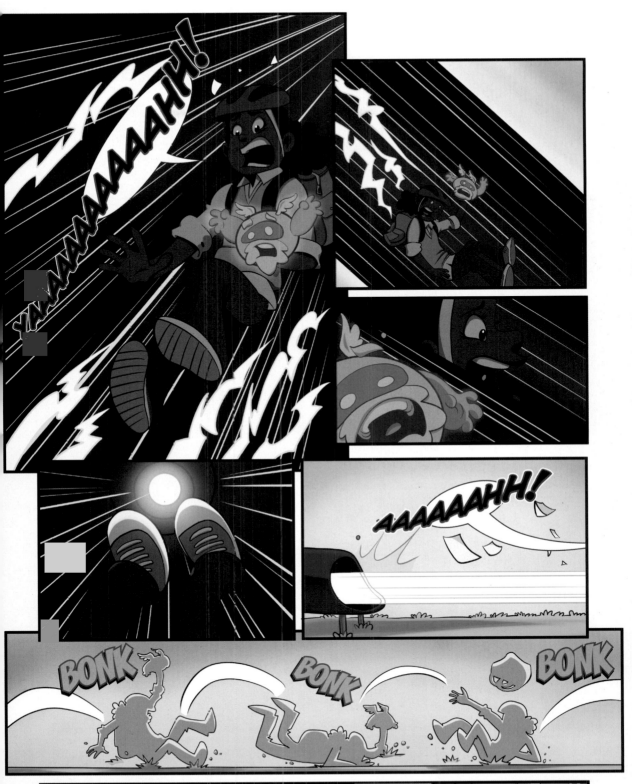

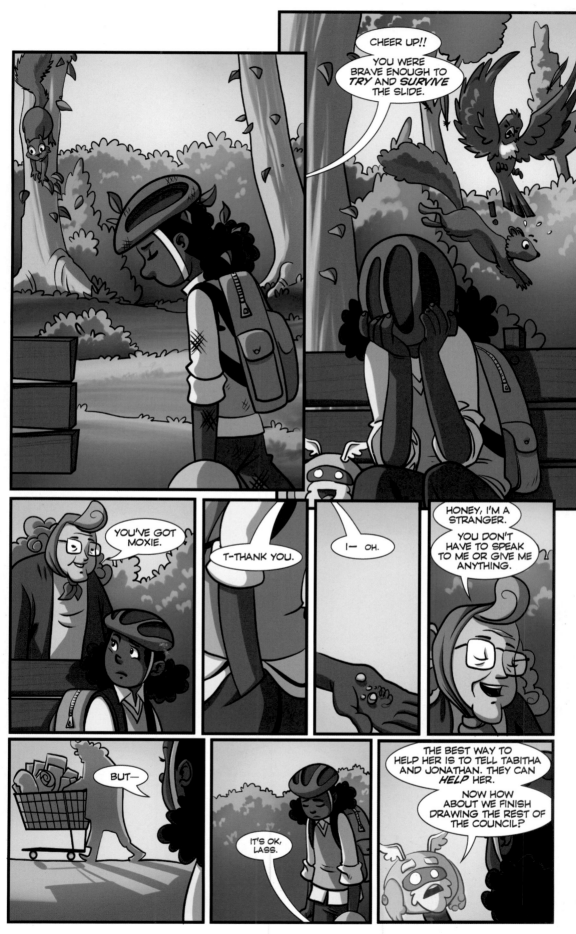

SEVERAL HOURS LATER.

THAT'S STERK?

HE LOOKS SCARY.

THAT'S THE POINT.

HE IS THE STRONGEST WARRIOR IN ALL OF VORGON. HE'S NOT SUPPOSED TO MAKE YOU FEEL WARM AND FUZZY.

<GIGGLE> BUT YOU'RE FUZZY.

HA HA...LET'S DRAW DELFI.

DELFI IS *VERY* MYSTERIOUS.

SHE WEARS A LONG ROBE WITH A HOOD, AND SHE HAS TWO HORNS.

YOU CALL *THAT* A ROBE?!

A ROBE! LIKE A CLOAK! SHE'S A MYSTERIOUS TRUTH TELLER.

OK, YOU KNOW WHAT...

70

I DIDN'T STEAL ANYTHING!

THE PIZZA WAS IN THE DUMPSTER.

COME BACK, BUM!

VAGRANT!

MEMBERS ONLY!

ASA, WE HAVE TO HELP HER!

AYE, LASS, BUT I CAN'T PUT YOU IN DANGER.

BUT THOSE PEOPLE HAVE PUT THAT POOR WOMEN IN DANGER—JUST FOR TAKING A PIZZA OUT OF THE TRASH.

ALL RIGHT THEN. LET'S *SAVE* HER!

BACK WHERE WE STARTED.

GRAB THE WOMAN'S BASKET, LASS.

Wobble Wobble

LITTLE GIRL, HOW ARE YOU RUNNING SO FAST?

I'M...UH...A TRACK STAR.

HOLD ON!

SWOOOOOOSH!!

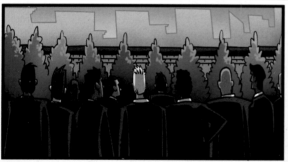

She wasn't a *member*.

Uh...asa...I thought...

Don't say one word.

Not one.

GASP

That was *amazing!*

You really *are* a track star.

Uh...yeah.

And you have a great lucky charm there.

You know...

...I HAVE A GOOD LUCK CHARM MYSELF.

I ALWAYS FIND THE BEST FOOD WHEN I TAKE HER ALONG WITH ME.

NEMA!

THAT'S NEMA?

BUT YOU SHOULD BE MORE CAREFUL.

IF PEOPLE SEE YOU WITH YOUR FRIEND, THEY MAY PUT YOU IN A PLACE WITH PADDED WALLS.

I KNOW THIS MAY SOUND STRANGE, BUT I WANTED TO ASK WHERE YOU GOT THAT PUPPET...OR MAYBE OTHERS LIKE IT.

WHY?

WHAT DO YOU WANT WITH MY PUPPET?

WELL, THERE IS A SET THAT...UH... BELONGED TO MY MOTHER, MY REAL MOTHER.

THEY GOT LOST. I WANTED TO GET THEM BACK.

WELL, I FOUND HER IN A TRASH BIN ON MAIN STREET.

SHE HAD BEEN THROWN AWAY. NO ONE WANTED HER, EXCEPT ME.

THEY TRIED TO TAKE HER AWAY AT...THE BAD PLACE...

...AND NOW I SUPPOSE YOU WANT HER TOO.

WELL, YOU CAN'T HAVE MY GOOD LUCK CHARM.

YOU KNOW, I SAW YOU DRAWING EARLIER.

ARE YOU A PRETTY GOOD ARTIST?

I DON'T KNOW.

LET'S SEE JUST HOW GOOD OF AN ARTIST YOU ARE.

I WANT YOU TO DRAW A PORTRAIT OF ME.

DRAW MY FUTURE.

WHERE DO YOU THINK I GO FROM HERE?

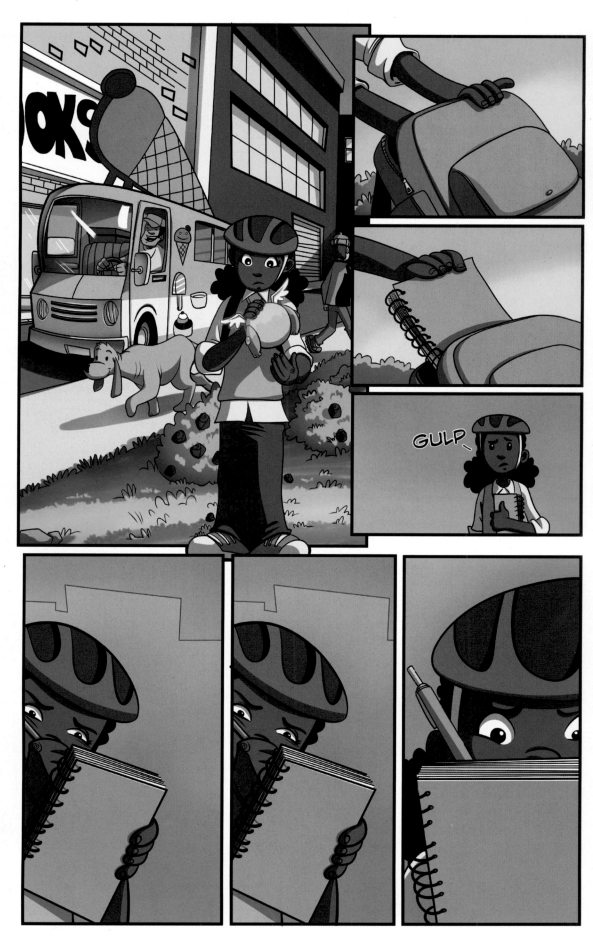

ASA, I THOUGHT YOU COULD FLY.

I CAN, BUT I GUESS MY POWERS HAVE CHANGED.

MAYBE, ALL THE NINES' POWERS HAVE CHANGED.

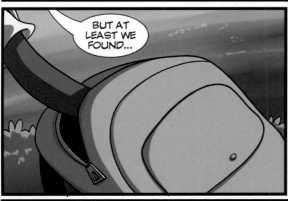

BUT AT LEAST WE FOUND...

...LOVELY, LOVELY NEMA.

YEAH.

OY!

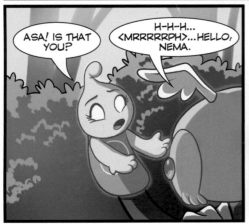

ASA! IS THAT YOU?

H-H-H... <MRRRRRPH>...HELLO, NEMA.

ASA, YOU'RE SO...

...FUZZY!

HAHAHAHAHA <SNORT>!

HEHEHE

Chapter Four
All That Glitters

SUNDAY MORNING. AUDREY'S ROOM.

SO, THERE WAS NUFFINK I COULD DO, YEAH.

NUFFINK?

HEKLA'S TWITS 'AD ME COLD.

WHIRL WHIRL

GONNA GET CAUGHT, YEAH.

AND ME A MEMBER OF THE NINE.

NEMA OF THE AMUNET... ...YOU HAVE BEEN INVITED TO LINGER IN A GILDED ROOM—

DRRRIIIIZZZZMM!

SWOOOSH!

BUT I WEREN'T HAVIN' NONE OF IT.

WELL, AIN'T THAT SOME—

POOF

KNOCK KNOCK

AUDREY, ARE YOU OK?

I HEARD SOME WEIRD NOISES.

NEMA, YOU TURNED ME INVISIBLE AGAIN!

UHHH....HOLD ON A MINUTE.

I JUST HAD SOME BAD DREAMS.

NO PROBS, LOVE.

JUST TAKE US OFF YOUR HANDS, YEAH.

KA-POOF

OH YEAH. GUESS I PANICKED.

OK... TABITHA. YOU CAN COME IN.

GOOD MORNING.

HOW ARE...

...YOU?

ROUGH NIGHT, HUH?

I...ER....

WELL, LET'S REPLACE THOSE BAD DREAMS WITH SOME GOOD THOUGHTS.

I'VE GOT A SURPRISE FOR YOU.

A SURPRISE?

TODAY IS *OUTRAGEOUSLY ZANY FUN PUPPET SHOW* DAY!

REALLY? MORE PUPPETS?

YEAH! IT'S AWESOME.

I WAS LUCKY TO GET A SHIRT LAST YEAR.

I THOUGHT YOU MIGHT LIKE TO WEAR IT.

UH...THANKS.

AUDREY...THIS IS MARVELOUS!

MAY I BORROW IT FOR A WHILE?

UH...I GUESS.

SCOUT'S HONOR. I PROMISE I WON'T LET ANYTHING HAPPEN TO IT.

OK.

DON'T WORRY ABOUT YOUR SKETCHBOOK, LASS.

SHE'LL TAKE GOOD CARE OF IT.

BUT MOST IMPORTANT, WE'RE GOING TO LOOK FOR OTHER PUPPETS.

YEAH. NO TELLIN' WHO WE MIGHT FIND.

IT MAY EVEN BE FUN.

AAAAAAAAAAAAAAAAAAA

AHHH!

HUH?

CAN I HOLD YOUR PUPPETS JUST FOR A MINUTE?

WE CAN'T STAY HERE.

THERE'S ANOTHER DOOR!

DON'T WORRY, LITTLE GIRL.

WE JUST WANT TO HOLD YOUR PUPPETS.

SHOULD WE TRY IT?

I DON'T SEE ANY OTHER OPTION.

THE EXIT IS JUST OUTSIDE.

BUT THERE ARE STILL CAST MEMBERS OUT THERE.

I HAVE AN IDEA.

AUDREY, YOU'RE SO TA—

WE HAVE TO LEAVE.

NOW.

THEATER

EVERYTHING OK?

NO COMMENT.

BAR 1

COULDN'T BE.

AUDREY, WHAT IS THIS?

STERK?

HOW DID THAT HAPPEN?

AT HOME. LATER.

THAT WAS A VERY CLEVER MANEUVER BACK THERE, STERK.

YEAH, HOW'D YA PULL THAT ONE OFF?

STERK, ARE YOU OK?

YOU...DON'T... KNOW....

NOT SO LOUD.

SIGH

YOU DON'T KNOW THE HUMILIATIONS, THE NUMEROUS OFFENSES, AND THE SHEER GLITTERED TERROR I HAVE HAD TO ENDURE.

I AM STERK! VORGON WARRIOR OF STRENGTH. NEVER DEFEATED IN COMBAT!

AND I HAVE BEEN MADE TO...TO...DANCE AND FROLIC UPON THE HANDS OF SHOW PEOPLE.

SNAAAAAAAARR

W-W-WHAT WAS THAT?

To be continued...

Three down, Six to go!

Fret not, Dear Reader, Audrey's adventures continue in
Book 2 as she unlocks the mysteries surrounding the rest
of the Magic Nine AND that terrifying sound.

BONUS STORY ONE

First Flight

Story by
Michelle Wright

Art by
Tracy Bailey

...IS WITH AVALLOC THE GREAT.

OOOOOO! THAT SOUNDS COOL.

WELL, YOU NEED TO KNOW THAT AVALLOC GAVE HIMSELF THE TITLE, AVALLOC THE GREAT. NO ONE ELSE DID.

HE WAS QUITE PUFFED ABOUT HIMSELF, HE WAS...

...SO MUCH SO THAT HE BRAGGED THAT HE WOULD FLY ALL THE WAY UP TO THE HIGHEST SUN OF VORGON.

THERE ARE *THREE*, YOU KNOW.

NO ONE BELIEVED HE COULD DO IT.

BUT AVALLOC VOWED THAT HE COULD...

...AND INDEED HE NEARLY MADE IT.

THE SUN HAD OTHER PLANS, HOWEVER, AND WOULDN'T BE VANQUISHED BY SUCH A BRAGGART.

THUMP!

IT FLUNG AVALLOC BACK TO THE GROUND AND INTO SHAME.

OF COURSE, AS A YOUNGLING ON THE VERGE OF MY FIRST FLIGHT, I ADMIRED AVALLOC'S STORY.

UNFORTUNATELY, I MISSED THE POINT OF IT ENTIRELY.

I IMAGINED MYSELF AS AVALLOC THE GREAT'S PROTÉGÉ, A MIGHTY ZEPHYR DESTINED FOR THE HIGH SUN.

I BRAGGED THAT MY FIRST FLIGHT WOULD TAKE ME THERE.

NO ONE BELIEVED ME...

...BUT I, TOO, VOWED TO SHOW THEM OTHERWISE.

THAT IS, I VOWED TO SHOW THEM, UNTIL I FIGURED OUT THAT I COULDN'T FLY.

MY FIRST FLIGHT WAS A DISASTER.

AND MY OVER CONFIDENCE VANISHED.

NO MATTER HOW HARD I TRIED AFTER THAT, I SIMPLY COULDN'T FLY.

I MIGHT NEVER HAVE LEARNED, HAD MY MOTHER NOT STEPPED IN.

SHE GAVE ME A FEATHER SHE SAID BELONGED TO AVALLOC THE GREAT.

SHE SAID IF I MIXED IT IN WITH MY OWN FEATHERS, AND CONCENTRATED ON STRETCHING MY WINGS AS FAR AS THEY COULD REACH, SHE SAID I WOULD FLY.

OF COURSE, I MISSED THE POINT OF THE STORY AGAIN.

THE FEATHER WAS MEANT ONLY TO REGAIN MY CONFIDENCE.

BUT I BELIEVED IF I DID JUST WHAT MY MOTHER SAID, I WOULD SUCCEED.

BONUS STORY TWO

Of Teeth And Top Knots

Story by
Michelle Wright

Art by
Tracy Bailey

OH...

...MY...

...GOSH!

CUTE, HUH?

YOUR CASE WORKER GAVE IT TO ME.

WHAT'S SO FUNNY?

NOTHING, LASS. IT'S CHARMING.

GUFFAW! NOTHING?

THAT'S ONE MAGNIFICENT *FANG!*

NOW, DON'T LOOK AT ME LIKE THAT, YEAH.

I LAUGH BECAUSE I'VE BEEN THERE MESELF.

EXCEPT I DIDN'T 'AVE A TUSK.

I HAD AN UNCOILED TOP KNOT.

VERY UNFORTUNATE INDEED.

IT WAS A TERRIBLE TIME.

SEE, BECAUSE EVERYONE ELSE HAD PERFECT COILS.

RRRIIIIIIIPPP!

EXCEPT FOR ME.

HA! HA! HA! HA! HA!

AND MY PEOPLE AREN'T THE MOST SENSITIVE TRIBE AROUND.

WHERE'D SHE GO?

I WAS LUCKY, THOUGH.

WHEW!

NOW, HOW DO I GET HOME?

I WAS JUST WONDERING THE SAME THING.

BECAUSE I MET A KINDRED SPIRIT.

THERE HE IS.

HA! HERE SHE IS.

SO WHAT ARE YOU GONNA DO?

LAUGH AT US SOME MORE?

UH...YEAH.

ONCE THEY REALIZED WE DIDN'T CARE ABOUT BEING RIDICULED ANYMORE, NO ONE BOTHERED US AGAIN.

YOU KNOW, IT'S REALLY NOT *THAT* BAD.

BLAH BLAH TICO BLAH BLAH BLAH....

OH, IT'S BAD ALL RIGHT.

YOU JUST SHOULDN'T WORRY ABOUT IT, YEAH.

End.

BONUS STORY THREE

Another Magic Nine

Story by
Michelle Wright

Art by
Tracy Bailey

LIFE IS STRANGE.

YOU'D THINK THAT GIVEN MY CURRENT EXISTENCE AS A PUPPET THAT I WOULD LONG FOR THE DAYS...

...WHEN I WAS STERK THE STRONG, A MEMBER OF THE COUNCIL OF NINE...

...WHEN I FACED THE EVIL QUEEN HEKLA WITHOUT FEAR.

BUT IF I COULD GO BACK IN TIME, I WOULD GO BACK TO MY EXISTENCE AS A YOUNGLING...

...LIKE LITTLE AUDREY HERE: CURIOUS AND QUESTING FOR FRIENDS, FOR THE MAGIC BETWEEN WORLDS.

I WOULD GO BACK TO THE TIME I SEARCHED FOR MY OWN MAGIC NINE...

...IN THE MOST UNEXPECTED OF PLACES...

...AMONG THE MARSH CREATURES, THAT VORGON TRIBE CONSIDERED INFERIOR TO EVERY OTHER CLAN ON THE PLANET.

I HAD NEVER SEEN ANYTHING LIKE IT.

BUT BY SPYING ON THE MARSH CREATURES...

UH-OH.

SNAP!

...I DIDN'T REALIZE THAT I WAS STEALING FROM THEM...

...STEALING THEIR MOST PRIVATE, HAPPY MOMENTS...

UMPH!

...SIMPLY BECAUSE I WAS CURIOUS...

...AND BECAUSE I DIDN'T RESPECT THE MARSH CREATURES ENOUGH TO LET THEM HAVE THEIR OWN JOYS.

I SHOULD HAVE KNOWN BETTER...

...BUT LIKE I SAID, I WAS YOUNG...

...AND FOOLISH...

...AND I HAD UNDERESTIMATED THE MARSH CREATURES.

WHEW!

SNAP!

I HAD UNDERESTIMATED THE MARSH CREATURES ENTIRELY...

...BUT NOT IN THE WAY YOU MAY THINK.

FOR ALL THE BAD RUMORS...

...THAT VORGON SPREAD ABOUT THE MARSH CREATURES...

...THEY ACTUALLY PROVED TO THE BE LOVELIEST...

...AND FUNNEST CREATURES...

...I HAD EVER KNOWN.

YAAAAAAAY!!!

THEY WERE MY MAGIC NINE.

THE NINE TO WHICH I WOULD HAPPILY RETURN.

End.

BONUS STORY FOUR

Planesong

Story by
Michelle Wright

Art by
Tracy Bailey

1966. AVONLEA FOSTER INSTITUTE.

MISS CHARLOTTE RENDON'S FIRST DAY AS A SOCIAL WORKER.

AVONLEA FOSTER INSTITUTION.

BECKY, CHARLIE, BE CAREFUL.

THUD!

YEAH. I'M GONNA HAVE TO CUT IT OUT.

IMPRESSIVE DESIGN, THOUGH.

YOU MUST KNOW YOUR WAY AROUND PAPER AIRPLANES.

YOU COULD SAY THAT.

CLIP!

DON'T MIND THOSE JOKERS.

HA! HA! HA! HA! HA! HA! HA!

HMMMM....

WOULD YOU HAPPEN TO BE OPEN—

HA! HA! HA! HA! HA! HA! HA!

End.

Huddleston • Moussa • Garcia

Huddleston • Moussa • Garcia

Huddleston • Moussa • Garcia

Huddleston • Moussa • Garcia

136

Huddleston • Moussa • Garcia

Huddleston · Moussa · Garcia

138

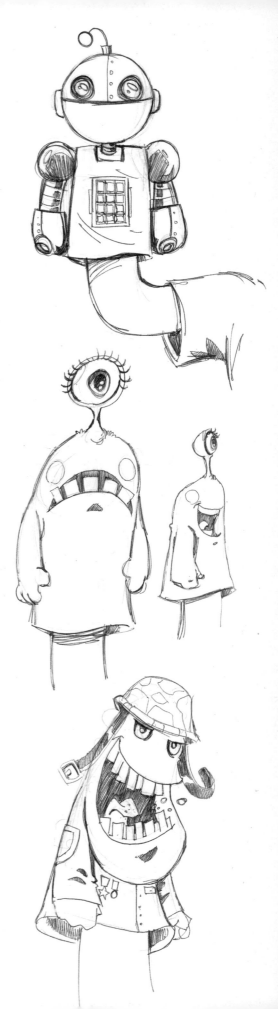

Bonus Art

By Courtney Huddleston

STERR

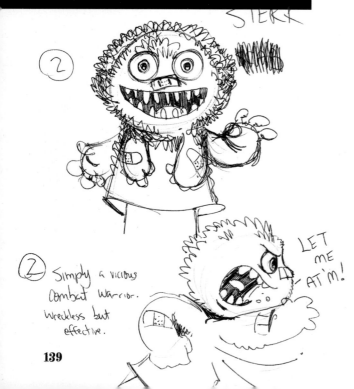

② Simply a vicious combat warrior. Wreckless but effective.

LET ME AT'M!

139